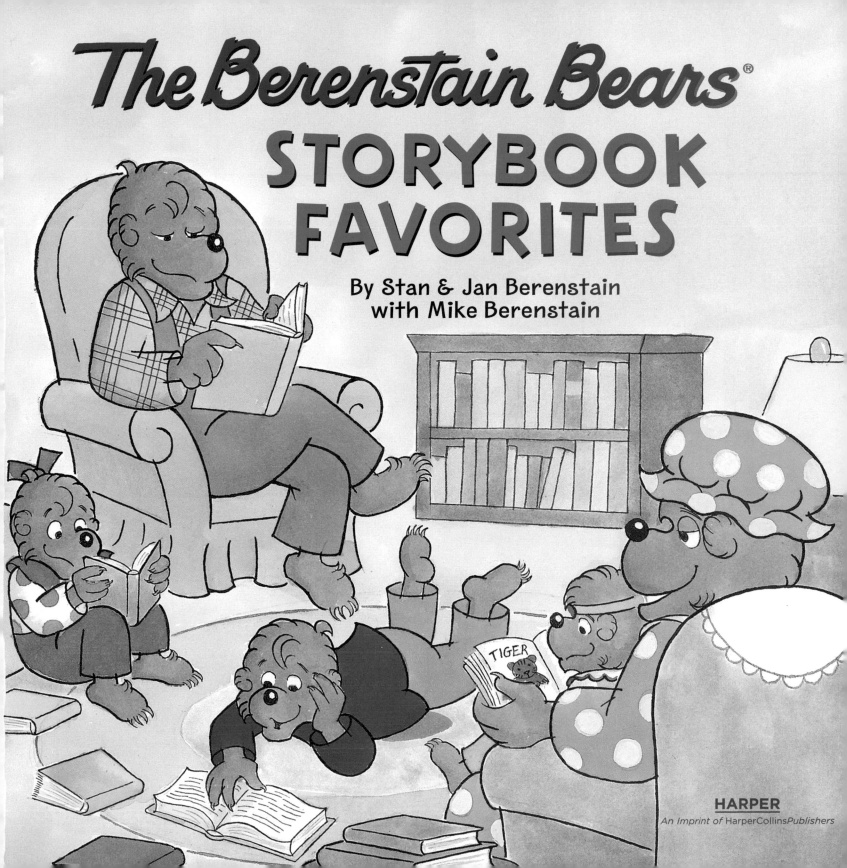

The Berenstain Bears®
STORYBOOK FAVORITES

By Stan & Jan Berenstain
with Mike Berenstain

HARPER
An Imprint of HarperCollins Publishers

TABLE OF CONTENTS

The Berenstain Bears' New Pup

Stan & Jan Berenstain

One day Mama and the cubs
went to Farmer Ben's farm.
They went there to buy
some fresh eggs.

"Look!" said Brother.

"There is a sign on Farmer Ben's barn door."

The sign said PUPS FOR SALE!

"Hmm," said Mama. "Farmer Ben's dog,

Queenie, must have had pups."

"Oh, Mama!" said Sister.

"May we have one? May we?

May we? Please?"

"We came to buy eggs," said Mama.

"Not a pup."

Farmer Ben was in the barn.

So was his dog, Queenie.

Queenie was in a box with her pups.

There were many pups.

Some of her pups were having lunch.

Some were sleeping.

12

One of them was playing

with a piece of straw.

"Oh," said Sister.

"I want that one!

He is so cute."

"That one is a she," said Farmer Ben.

"How can you tell?" asked Brother.

"There are ways," said Farmer Ben.

"Now, cubs," said Mama,

"buying eggs is one thing.

Buying a pup is quite another."

"Oh, Mama," said the cubs,

"may we have her?

May we? May we? Please?"

"A pup is not just something

you have," said Mama.

"A pup is something

you have to take care of."

"We will take care of her!"

said the cubs.

"A pup is something you have to clean up after," said Mama. "We will clean up after her," said the cubs.

"A pup likes to get into things,"

said Mama.

"We will watch her every second!"

said the cubs.

Farmer Ben picked up the pup

that was playing with the straw.

He put her in Mama's hands.

The pup looked into
Mama's eyes.

The pup licked
Mama's nose.

The pup wagged her tail…
and Mama's heart melted!

On the way home

they named the pup Little Lady.

They named her "little"

because she was little.

They named her "lady"

because she was a she.

"Yum!" said Papa Bear

when they got home.

"A dozen farm-fresh eggs!"

"And one farm-fresh pup!"

said Sister Bear.

Mama was right about Little Lady.

She did have to be cleaned up after.

She left a puddle in one corner…

and a calling card in another.

And she did like to get into things.

She got into Mama's baking flour.

Cough! Cough! Cough!

She got into Papa's fishing tackle.

What a tangle!

She got into Farmer Ben's

farm-fresh eggs.

What a mess!

"Hmm," said Mama.

"I am going back to Farmer Ben's."

"You're not going to take

Little Lady back to Farmer Ben's?"

cried Sister.

"No," said Mama.

"I am just going to get another dozen eggs."

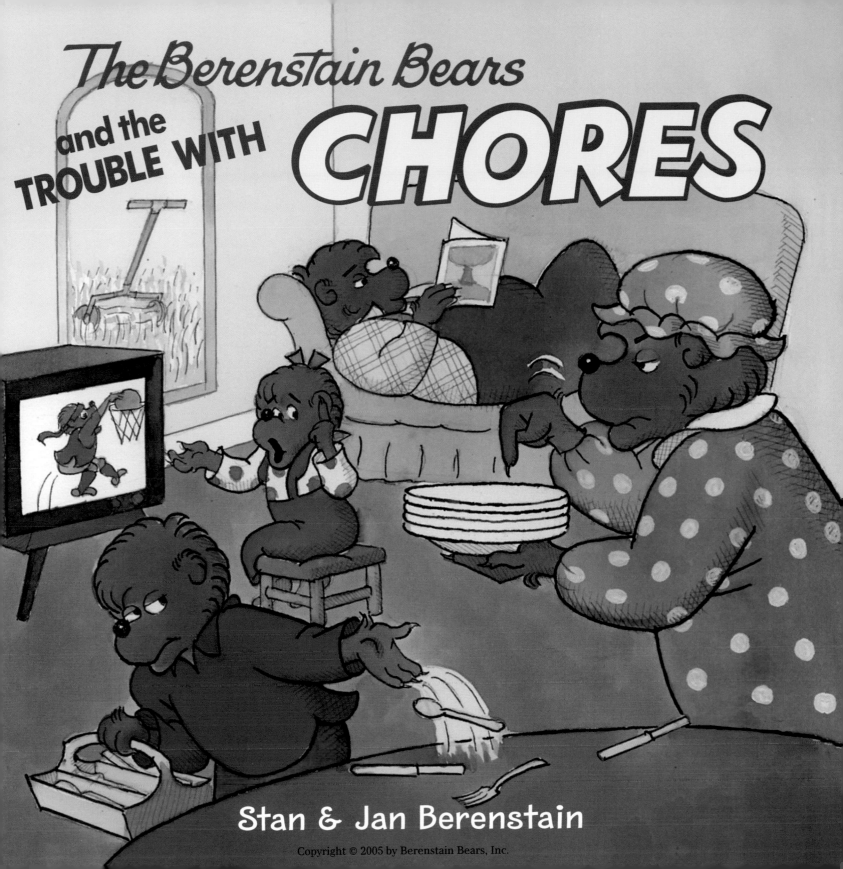

The Berenstain Bears and the TROUBLE WITH CHORES

Stan & Jan Berenstain

The Berenstain Bears
and the
TROUBLE WITH
CHORES

When asked to do something that they hate, most bears will procrastinate.

THINGS TO DO

Set the table
clear away dishes
Empty waste baskets
Put out trash
Cut grass
Coil garden hose
Clean up messy room
Empty vacuum
Pick up toys
Rake leaves
Sweep steps

Brother and Sister Bear were good about most things.

They kept up with their schoolwork.

They wore their safety helmets when they went biking and skateboarding.

They said "please" and "thank you" without being prompted.

Papa Bear was good about most things, too.
He helped the cubs with their homework.

He kept his tools sharp and
shipshape.

He was always ready to help
a neighbor.

But there was one thing the cubs and Papa were not good about—that was chores.

It wasn't that Papa and the cubs didn't want to do their chores. It was just that they always seemed to have reasons not to do them.

And they had such good excuses.

"You're right, my dear," said Papa. "The grass does need cutting. But a mama spider has spun a wonderful web on the lawn mower and I haven't the heart to put all her hard work to waste."

"Mama," said Brother, "may I skip setting the table tonight? There's a TV show on the ice age, and I have to do a report on the Beast of Baluchistan."

"Mama," said Sister, "I know it's my week to clean up Little Lady's calling cards. It's just that I'm waiting for them to dry. They'll be easier to scoop up that way."

There was also the endless bickering about who did what.

"Why is it," complained Sister, "that Brother gets the easy jobs, like setting the table, and I get the yucky ones, like scraping the plates into the garbage?"

"Easy? *Easy?*" protested Brother. "Setting that table is hard! You've got to remember where everything goes—the knives, the spoons, the forks!"

"Wanna trade?" asked Sister. "No, thanks," said Brother. So it went: argue, argue, bicker, bicker.

Mama sighed.

If only Papa and the cubs were as good at doing their chores as they were at arguing about them, life would be a lot easier.

And speaking of easier, thought Mama, *instead of nagging them about chores, it would be a lot easier to do them myself.*

And that's what she did.
She set and cleared the table.

She cleaned up after
Little Lady.

She chased the dust
bunnies from under
the furniture.

There was also baby Honey to take care of—

not to mention the cubs' messy room.

The cubs did pick up and put away—sometimes.

Papa did cut the grass—occasionally.

48

And the cubs did chase
the dust bunnies—
once in a while.

But when it comes to chores—
sometimes, occasionally, and
once in a while don't count.

Not surprisingly, things began to slide. Everybody got
a little grouchy—especially Mama.

Something had to be done. But what?

Papa decided to call a family meeting. "My dear," he said.
"I've been thinking."

"Yes?" said Mama.

"What I've been thinking," he continued, "is that we might
want to relax a bit, to ease
up on the chores a little."

"Oh?" said Mama.

"Yes," said Papa. "There's a lot more to life than chores. There's walking in the sunshine, enjoying Mother Nature, and fishing in the old fishing hole."

"There's riding bikes," said Brother.

"And jumping rope," said Sister.

Then, to Papa and the cubs' great surprise, Mama said, "You know something? I think you're absolutely right."

"You do?" said Papa.

"I certainly do," said Mama with a sly gleam in her eye. "I've been so concerned with the house that I haven't been to my quilting club for weeks. And with the flower show coming up, I should be preparing my exhibit."

Not worrying about spiderwebs and dust bunnies worked pretty well at first. There were a few bad moments—like when baby Honey almost ate a bug.

But Mama was her smiling self again. She got back into quilting and began work on her flower show exhibit. "I was thinking of combining Shasta daisies and Silver Moon roses. What do you think, dear?" she asked.

"Sounds fine to me," said Papa, who was working on his fishing gear.

"Mama," said Sister. "I'm growing this grapefruit plant for school and there are so many dishes in the kitchen sink that I can't water it."

"No problem," said Mama. "Just water it in the bathroom upstairs."

Sister stomped upstairs with her grapefruit plant.

"Mama," said Brother, "I left my marbles on the floor and now they're gone!"

"Goodness!" said Mama. "I must have sucked them up with the vacuum. I do have to vacuum once in a while."

"But one of them was my best shooter!" said Brother.

"Oh, I'm sure you can find them by emptying the vacuum bag," said Mama.

"But . . . but . . . but . . ." sputtered Brother.

"Now if you'll excuse me," said Mama. "I'm off to my quilting club."

Some household tasks got done. Beds got made—more or less. Meals got served—sort of. But bit by bit, messy build-up began to take over the tree house.

Wet towels piled up in the bathroom.

Fruit flies hovered over dishes in the kitchen sink.

The pictures on the wall got crookeder and crookeder, and there was a whole army of dust bunnies under the sofa.

There were so many burnt crumbs
in the bottom of the toaster oven
that the whole kitchen smelled
burnt.

A strange green mold
grew on the shower curtain,

and a thousand-legger came swimming
toward Sister in the bathtub.

Yes, Brother was having fun riding his bike. Sister was having fun jumping rope.

Papa brought home some fine fish, and Mama finished her beautiful new quilt.

But living in all that messy build-up wasn't much fun. And one day when Mama was off at the garden club, Papa decided to call another meeting. No sooner had the meeting been called to order than everybody was talking at once—and they were all saying the same thing: "WE'VE GOT TO DO SOMETHING ABOUT THIS AWFUL MESS!"

And they did.

They picked up all the wet towels.

They got the dishes out of the sink.

They straightened the pictures.

They cleaned out
the toaster oven,
banished the
dust bunnies,
and scrubbed
the shower
curtain.
Then they sat down,
exhausted and pleased,
and waited
for Mama to
come home.

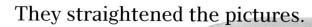

"Well," she said when she returned, "everything is set for the flower show. And I think there's a good chance I may win an award." Papa and the cubs waited for her to notice what they had done. But all Mama did was take off her yellow "going out" hat and put on her blue "at home" duster.

"Mama," said Sister, "haven't you noticed anything?"
Mama looked around and smiled. "You mean how the
whole house is neat and clean and all the chores are
done—yes, I noticed."

With that, she gathered the cubs into a big bear
hug and gave Papa a great big kiss.

The Berenstain Bears
and the
WISHING STAR

Stan & Jan
Berenstain

One day the Bear family went to the mall.

They passed the toy store.

They looked in the toy store window.

"What a beautiful teddy bear!" said Sister.

"It's okay," said Brother.

"If you like teddies."

"Well, I do," said Sister,

"and I *love* that teddy."

Hmm, thought Papa,

Sister's birthday is coming.

Mama had the same thought.

That night the cubs were doing their homework.

Brother was making a map of Bear Country.

Sister was doing numbers homework.

She was not doing well with numbers.

She got a C on her last report card.

Papa was helping her.

She wanted to get a B or even an A.

Soon it was bedtime.

"Look!" said Mama.

"The wishing star."

"What is the wishing star?"

asked Sister.

"It is the first star that comes

out at night," said Mama.

"You can wish upon it."

Then Mama said the wishing star rhyme:

"Star light, star bright,

first star I see tonight.

I wish I may, I wish I might

have the wish I wish tonight."

"What happens then?" asked Sister.

"If you wish hard," said Mama,

"and you do not tell anyone your wish,

it *might* come true."

"I'm going to try it," said Sister.

She said the rhyme:

"Star light, star bright,

first star I see tonight.

I wish I may, I wish I might

have the wish I wish tonight."

Then Sister fell asleep.

She dreamed of the beautiful teddy.

Sister's birthday came.

She got the teddy for her birthday.

"I got my wish! I got my wish! she cried.

After supper and birthday cake,

Sister and Brother did their homework.

Brother was still working on his map.

Sister was still working on numbers.

Getting a B or even an A would be so nice,

she thought.

That night Sister made another wish.

She said the wishing rhyme again.

Then she fell asleep and dreamed.

She dreamed about getting a B or even an A.

Sister got her report card the next day.

She got an A for numbers.

"I got my wish! I got my wish!" she cried.

REPORT CARD
Sister Bear

NUMBERS A

LANGUAGE B+

SPELLING A

Brother got a good report card, too.

They got a reward.

They were allowed to stay up

and watch a special TV show.

STAY
TUNED

It was about a pony—

a beautiful, white pony.

Sister fell in love with that pony.

That night she said the wishing rhyme again:

"Star light, star bright,

first star I see tonight.

I wish I may, I wish I might

have the wish I wish tonight."

Then she went to sleep and dreamed.

She dreamed about the beautiful pony.

The next morning
she woke up early.
She ran downstairs.

She ran outside to look for her new pony.

She looked all over.

It wasn't tied to the fence.

It wasn't in the shed.

It wasn't anywhere.

Sister was very sad when she came back.

"What's the matter?" asked Brother.

"I did not get my wish," said Sister.

"What did you wish for?" asked Brother.

"I'm not supposed to tell," said Sister.

"You can tell if you don't

get your wish," said Brother.

"I wished for a beautiful, white pony,"
Sister said.

"Oh," said Brother. "You know, Sis,

you have to be careful with the wishing star.

If you are greedy or ask for too much,

the wishing star may not hear you."

"I got my first wish," said Sister.

"It was your birthday," Brother said.

"I got my second wish," said Sister.

"You worked hard for that A," said Brother,

"but a pony? I don't know about that, Sis."

Sister thought about that.

Then she smiled and said,

"Well, anyway, two out of three isn't bad."

The Berenstain Bears
and TOO MUCH
CAR TRIP

Stan & Jan Berenstain

The Berenstain Bears
and
TOO MUCH
CAR TRIP

Never take cubs on long drives
is a pretty good tip.
But there may come a time
when it's all worth the trip.

The Berenstain Bears
and
TOO MUCH
CAR TRIP

Stan & Jan Berenstain

It was just about vacation time for the Bear Family. Brother and Sister Bear knew where *they* wanted to go on vacation. Brother's choice was Great Grizzlyland. "Cousin Fred's been there twice," he said. "He says it has all the biggest, steepest, fastest rides!"

Sister had a different idea. She wanted to go to Wild White Water Kingdom. "Lizzy went there last year and she says it's awesome! It's got a white water ride where everybody has to wear a bathing suit. It's got a pool that makes a huge wave, a corkscrew waterslide and . . ."

"I'm sure those places are fun," interrupted Papa Bear, "but we're going on a different sort of vacation this year."

"Oh?" said Brother. "Where are we going?"

"We're going on a car trip," said Papa. "As a matter of fact, I'm planning it right now on this road map." He was seated at the dining room table. He had a big map spread out on it.

"A car trip?" said the cubs. That's what the cubs
said. But that's not what they were thinking. What
they were thinking was: *Oh no, not a car trip! Not
a long, boring car trip!*

"A car trip to where?" asked Brother.

"Your mother and I have decided that it's time
for you two to see more of the country," said Papa.

Sister was puzzled. "What country is that?" she asked.

Papa looked up from the map. "Why, Bear Country, of course," he said.

"What kind of vacation is that?" asked Brother. "We can see Bear Country any old time."

"Yeah," said Sister. "We can just look out the window."

"Besides," said Brother, "what's there to see?"

"There's a great deal to see," said Papa. "And a great deal more to appreciate. So why don't you just sit there beside me and I'll show you where we're going on this map." They climbed up on chairs beside Papa and looked at the map.

It didn't look like much of a vacation to the cubs. It looked like just what it was—a big, boring map.

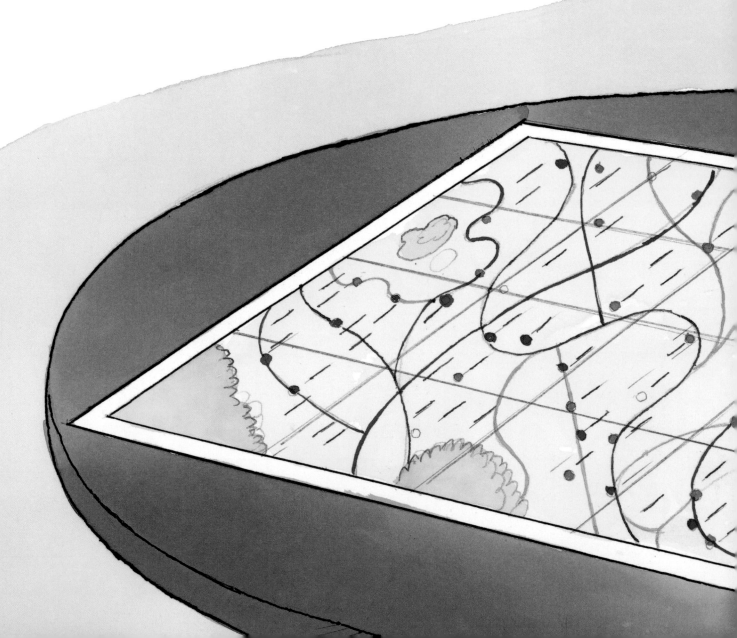

"Well, what do you two think of our vacation plans?" asked Mama Bear, coming into the room with baby Honey. "Is Honey coming with us on this car trip?" asked Sister. "Goodness no," said Mama. "She's not old enough to appreciate a trip like this. I've arranged for Honey to stay with Gramps and Gran while we're away."

Lucky Honey! thought the cubs. *She gets to have fun with Gramps and Gran while we have to go on a long, boring car trip.*

"You know," said Brother, "baby Honey is a lot of work. Why don't we stay and help Gramps and Gran while you two go on the car trip?"

Mama and Papa didn't think that was such a good idea.

They packed up and left early the next morning. After saying their good-byes to baby Honey, Gramps, and Gran, they headed for the open road.

Mama knew how the cubs felt, so she brought along things for them to do during the trip. She brought crayons, a book of mazes, and some board games. But the cubs were so determined to be bored that they ignored the things Mama had brought. They just sat in the back of the car with their arms folded.

Since they were looking straight ahead, the cubs didn't notice that the country around them was changing. The trees were getting bigger and wilder. The land was getting craggier. They didn't even notice the wide blue sky filled with great white clouds sailing and scudding over the broad country.

But there was something they did notice—a distant roaring sound. It's hard to stay bored when there's a distant roaring sound that's getting louder and louder. "What's that roaring sound?" asked Brother.

"That's Honeymoon Falls," said Mama. "It's where Papa and I spent our honeymoon."

Just then they turned a corner and there it was. Tons of water were pouring over a cliff and crashing into the river below.

115

Brother and Sister forgot all about being bored and said, "Wow!" They parked the car and went to Honeymoon Point overlooking the falls.

They had to rent slickers to keep from getting drenched. "*I BET THEY DON'T HAVE ANYTHING LIKE THIS AT WILD WHITE WATER KINGDOM!*" shouted Sister over the roar.

"There's something I don't quite understand, Mama," she added as they headed back to the car. "If you were here on your honeymoon, how come I don't remember it?" Mama and Papa just looked at each other as Brother whispered, "We weren't even born yet, silly!"

That gave Sister something to think about on the next leg of their car trip.

"Hey, look!" shouted Brother. "Soldiers fighting! They're shooting at each other!"

"Nothing to worry about, Son," said Papa. "They're just shooting blanks. They're reenactors."

"Huh? What's reenactors?" asked Brother.

"They're folks that act out important things that happened a long time ago."

"What are they *re-en-act-ing*?" asked Sister.

Papa looked at the map. "Hmm. I'd say it's the Battle of Beadle Creek. See that stream? That's Beadle Creek."

"Who was doing the fighting?" asked Brother.

"Folks just like us," said Papa.

"What were they fighting about?" asked Sister.

"You know, countries don't just happen," said Papa. "Folks have to make them happen. And sometimes there's trouble. That's what the reenactors want us to think about. Sometimes you can learn from the past and do a better job in the future. Look over there, behind that low wall."

The cubs looked.

"See those stones?" asked Papa. "They mark the graves of the soldiers who fell in battle."

Brother started to say "Wow!" but nothing came out. Sister took hold of Mama's hand and leaned against her.

Back on the road they went up, up, uphill for a long time. They passed a sign that said ELEVATION 7,610 FT.

"What's that sign mean?" asked Brother.

"We're in the Great Grizzly Mountains and that's how high we are," said Mama.

120

That's when they turned a corner and found themselves looking down the steepest, narrowest, windingest road they had ever seen. The wind rushed past as they plunged down the mountain.

"Whew!" said Brother when they got to the bottom. "I bet they don't have anything like that at Great Grizzlyland."

"That's a pretty safe bet," said Papa.

121

They passed a sign that said NOW ENTERING BEAR COUNTRY NATIONAL PARK: HOME OF MOUNT GRIZZMORE. "What's a national park, Mama?" asked Sister.

"It's a park that belongs to the whole country," said Mama.

"What's Mount Grizzmore?" asked Brother.

"It's a very special mountain," said Papa.

"What's special about it?" asked Sister.

"You'll see in a minute, dear," said Mama.

Mount Grizzmore came into view
as they came out of a clump of trees.
And it really *was* special. It had three
enormous faces carved into its side.

"Who are they?" asked Brother from the observation area.
"They're some of the great heroes of Bear Country history," said Papa. "Their faces are carved in the mountain so we won't forget them."
Brother and Sister looked up at the great faces.

124

A picture came into Brother Bear's mind's eye. It showed the three historic faces, but there was another one, too.

126

It was the face of Brother Bear. "A penny for your thoughts, Son," said Papa.

"Er, uh . . . I was just thinking how this trip is a lot different from what I expected," he said.

Of course, there was a lot more that happened during the Bear family's car trip.

There were spilled drinks,

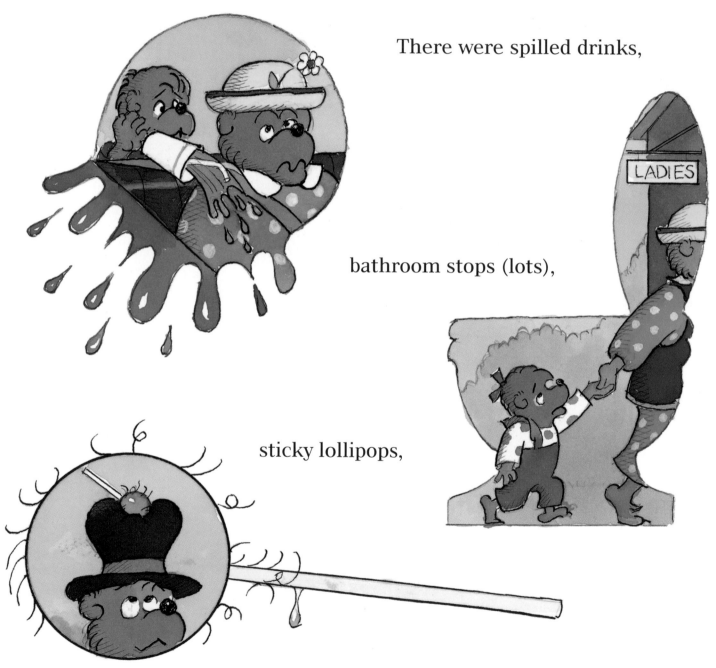

bathroom stops (lots),

sticky lollipops,

souvenir stops,

motel stops,

and all the other things that usually go with
car trips. But that's not what the cubs remembered.
What they remembered was the big sky,
the great falls, the mighty mountains, the little
graveyard at Beadle Creek, and the heroes of
Bear Country's history in the side of a mountain.

Baby Honey Bear was asleep when they
picked her up at Gramps and Gran's
and headed home. "You know something,
Papa," said Brother as they climbed
the steps of the tree house. "We ought
to take Honey on a car trip sometime—
when she's old enough to appreciate it,
of course."

"Of course," said Papa.

The Berenstain Bears' SEASHORE TREASURE

PIRATES COVE

Stan & Jan Berenstain

The Bear family was going to the seashore.
They were going across a bridge.

The bridge went to Laughing Gull Island.

It was called Laughing Gull Island

because so many laughing gulls lived there.

"*Ha! Ha! Ha!*" cried the laughing gulls

as they sailed across the sky.

"Will we be there soon?" asked Sister Bear.

"Yes," said Papa Bear.

"Do you see that house on the beach?

That is where we are going to stay."

The Bear family unpacked the car.

They carried their things into the house.

Brother, Sister, and Papa Bear

put on their swimsuits.

Mama decided to wait until later.

"Come, Papa," said Brother.

"Let's go to the beach."

"Hmm," said Papa.

"I found something in the closet."

"What is it?" asked Brother.

"It is a map," said Papa.

"An old pirate treasure map."

"Really, my dear," said Mama.

"It says this place used to be called

Pirates Cove!" said Papa.

"It says that pirates buried their booty here."

"What is booty, Papa?" asked Sister.

"It is treasure," said Papa. "Pirate treasure.

You know—gold, silver, diamonds, and rubies."

"Now, really, my dear," said Mama.

"Do you think the map is real?" asked Brother.

"There's only one way to find out,"

said Papa. "Follow me."

Papa got a shovel.

They went down to the beach.

It was a bright sunny day.

The sea sparkled.

Waves crashed upon the shore.

"*Ha! Ha! Ha!*" cried the laughing gulls.

Papa began to dig.

The cubs splashed in the sea.

"Have you found any treasure yet, Papa?"

asked Brother.

"Not so far," said Papa.

"All I have found are some old shells."

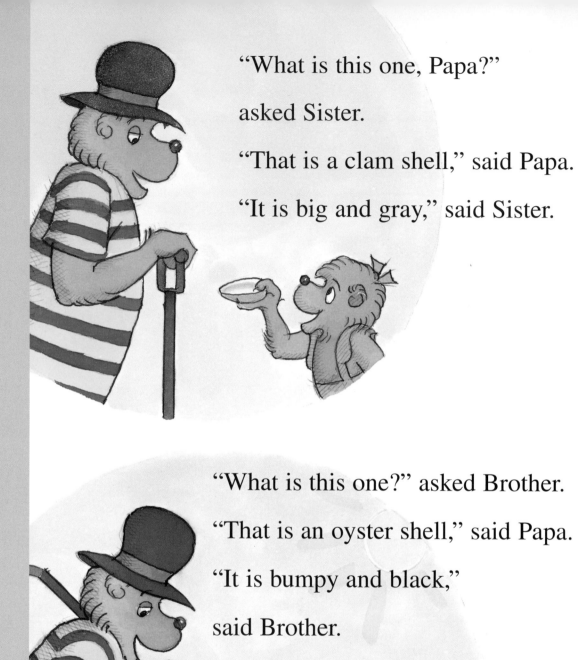

"What is this one, Papa?"
asked Sister.

"That is a clam shell," said Papa.

"It is big and gray," said Sister.

"What is this one?" asked Brother.

"That is an oyster shell," said Papa.

"It is bumpy and black,"

said Brother.

Papa looked at the treasure map.

"Hmm," he said. "This must not be the right spot."

He moved to another spot

and dug some more.

"Any treasure yet, Papa?"

asked Brother.

"No, just more old shells," said Papa.

"What is this one?"

asked Brother.

"That is a scallop shell," said Papa.

"It is pretty and pink,"

said Sister.

"What are shells for?" asked Brother.

"Shells are the homes of some sea animals," said Papa.

"The clam shell was the home of a clam.

The oyster shell was the home of an oyster.

The scallop shell was the home of a scallop."

The sun shone down. The sea sparkled.

Waves crashed upon the shore.

"*Ha! Ha! Ha!*" cried the laughing gulls.

"Papa, what happened to the clam, the oyster, and the scallop?" asked Sister.

"I guess maybe the laughing gulls got them," said Papa.

Papa looked at the map again.

"Hmm," he said. "This must not be the right spot."

He went to another spot and dug some more.

"Any treasure yet, Papa?" asked Sister.

"I'm afraid not," said Papa.

"Just some more old shells."

"You know something?" said Papa.

"Digging for treasure is hot work!"

154

"*Ha! Ha! Ha!*" cried the laughing gulls.

"Hmm," said Papa.

"Do you think those gulls are laughing at us

and our treasure hunt?"

"No way!" said Brother.

"We came looking for treasure
and we found it.

We found *the treasure of the sea*!"

"That's right," said Sister.

"A whole bucket full!"

"Time for a dip!" said Papa.

After they cooled off

they headed back to the house

to show Mama their treasure.

"Papa," said Brother, "what are you going to do with the treasure map?"

"Hmm," said Papa, "I may just leave it in the closet for the next papa bear."

The Berenstain Bears
SICK DAYS

Jan & Mike Berenstain

When cubs get sick
and stay home from school
"more work for Mama"
is the general rule.

The Berenstain Bears
SICK DAYS

Jan & Mike Berenstain

The morning sun was just peeking over the treetops when Mama Bear put two steaming hot bowls of oatmeal on the table, ready for Brother and Sister when they came down for breakfast. There were two smiley faces made of raisins on the oatmeal to make it more fun to eat.

Mama heard someone clumping loudly down the stairs. It was Brother Bear, still half asleep.

"Where's Sister?" asked Mama, a little surprised. Sister was usually up bright and early.

"She's still in bed," said Brother with a yawn.

"But she'll miss the bus!" said Mama.

"That's what I told her," Brother said, starting to eat his oatmeal. He tried to get one raisin in each spoonful to make them last. "But she just sort of groaned and rolled over."

That didn't sound like the Sister Bear Mama knew.

"Papa," said Mama, "will you please keep an eye on Honey Bear while I go to check on Sister?"

"Sure thing," said Papa, leaning over his *Bear Country News* to catch some drips under Honey Bear's chin.

Mama went upstairs and looked into Sister's room. Sister was still in bed and almost invisible under the blankets.

"Sister!" called Mama softly. "It's time to get up!"

But Sister just groaned.

"Oh, dear!" said Mama and gently pulled the covers down.

Sister gazed up at her drowsily.

"Mama," said Sister in a low, croaky sort of voice, "I don't feel so good."

Mama felt Sister's forehead. It was quite hot.

"I'm afraid you may have a fever, Sister," said Mama, concerned. "I'll be right back with a thermometer."

Mama hurried to the bathroom and back again. It was the first of the hurrying she would do that day.

"Put this under your tongue and hold it there," Mama said, shaking down the thermometer. She bustled around the room, straightening up, then took the thermometer out of Sister's mouth.

"Hmm!" said Mama. "One hundred degrees! You do have a temperature. You'll have to stay home from school today."

"I don't feel so good," was all that Sister could manage to say in her low, scratchy voice.

While Mama was giving Sister some pills for her fever and getting her to drink a glass of water, Papa came in with Honey Bear.

"Brother's off to school," said Papa. "But he said to tell you that he hopes you feel better."

"Thanks," croaked Sister.

"We hope you feel better, too," said Papa, kissing Sister on the head.

"Bedder!" said Honey.

Sister managed a little smile.

"I've got to deliver an order of new chairs this morning," said Papa, handing Honey over to Mama. "I'm afraid you'll have to hold down the fort on your own."

"Don't worry," said Mama with a weary smile. "I'll manage."

And manage she did.

First, Mama took Honey downstairs and put her in her playpen with some toys. After washing up the breakfast dishes, she did some laundry. Then she went back upstairs to help Sister get out of bed and walk down the hall to the bathroom.

Honey Bear started yelling, so Mama trotted downstairs to give her some new toys. After that Mama made up a tray with graham crackers and milk in case Sister felt hungry. While Mama was upstairs, she heard Honey yelling again and dashed back down to change her. Now it was time to put the laundry in the dryer. Mama was getting a bit tired.

After lunch, Mama put Honey Bear down for a nap. *Time for a rest*, she thought.

But just as she sat down with a cup of tea and a copy of *The Lady Bear's Journal*, Sister showed up at the bottom of the stairs, trailing her blanket like a cape.

"Mama," said Sister, "I'm bored. I don't have anything to do. Can I watch some TV?"

"Do you really feel well enough to be out of bed?" asked Mama.

"I think so," said Sister, curling up on the sofa. "I feel a lot better now."

"Well, all right then," said Mama, turning on the TV. "You can watch for a little while."

After making sure Sister was comfortable, Mama went into the kitchen to get something out of the freezer for dinner.

Sister enjoyed lying on the sofa watching TV. She was wrapped in her blanket and propped up on soft pillows. She watched a DVD of *The Bear of the Rings*, one of her favorites. The sofa reminded her of the big castle in the movie.

Sister decided that her castle needed to be stronger in case the servants of the Wicked Bear attacked.

Sister gathered cushions from all the chairs in the room and piled them up around the sofa. She got a broom out of the closet and pretended it was a catapult to shoot pillows at the attacking army. She shot a pillow right across the room and knocked one of Mama's potted plants on the floor. The dirt from the plant went everywhere.

"I see you're feeling *much* better!" said Mama, looking at the damage. "If you're well enough to knock over my plants, you're well enough to help me clean up."

When they were finished, Sister was worn out. She was still sick, after all. She lay down on the sofa and took a little nap.

But Mama didn't get a moment's peace because Honey Bear woke up from her nap and wanted to play.

Mama looked up at the clock. It was nearly time for Brother to come home from school, and Mama always liked to have milk and cookies ready for the cubs to eat before they started their homework.

"Oh, my aching back!" groaned Mama, getting up from the floor and going into the kitchen.

A few minutes later, Brother Bear came home.

"Hi, Mama!" he called, tossing his book bag on a chair. "How's Sister?"

"Much better, thank you!" Sister answered from the living room. She was awake again and nearly feeling like her old self.

"That's good news," said Brother, "because I brought you your homework."

"But, I can't do homework!" said Sister. "I'm sick!"

"You just said you were much better," Mama pointed out, coming in with milk and cookies on a tray.

"Well, yes," admitted Sister, "but not *that* much better."

"I think you'd better do your homework anyway," said Mama. "I don't think you're going to be sick enough to stay home from school tomorrow."

"Aw, Mama!" Sister sighed. But she did her homework all the same.

When Papa came home from making his furniture deliveries, he found Brother and Sister hard at work on their homework. Honey Bear was busily knocking down the castle of blocks on the floor, and Mama Bear was sitting at the kitchen table, holding her head in her hands.

"Whatever's the matter?" asked Papa, concerned.
"I don't feel so good," said Mama in a low, croaky sort of voice.

That night Mama went to sleep early while Papa put the cubs to bed by himself.

"What's wrong with Mama?" asked Sister as Papa tucked her in.

"She has a little fever," he told her, kissing her goodnight. "She probably has a touch of what you had today. I'm sure she'll get over it in a day or two, just like you did."

"Poor Mama," said Brother. "She can't even stay home from school. She doesn't go to school!"

"Don't worry," said Papa, turning out the light. "I'll take good care of both Mama and Honey tomorrow. Mama will be able to stay home from *home* for a day!"

And that is exactly what Mama Bear did.

HARPER
An Imprint of HarperCollinsPublishers   www.harpercollinschildrens.com   Illustrations © Berenstain Publishing, Inc.